MW00366175

Curlylocks and the Three Bears

A Play

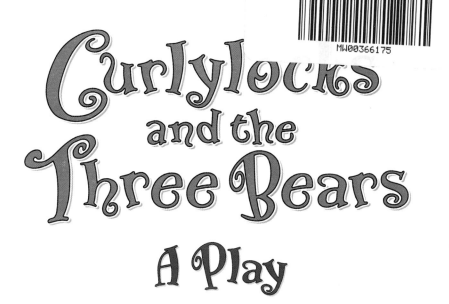

Cynthia Rider

Illustrated by Melanie Mansfield

Rigby

The Characters

Curlylocks

Father Bear

Mother Bear

Baby Bear

Narrator: The three bears are in the kitchen.

Father Bear: I have made some pizza.

Baby Bear: I want some cake, too!

Mother Bear: We can go and get some cake!

Narrator: The three bears go out.

3

Narrator: Curlylocks comes in.

Curlylocks: Mmmm. I want some pizza!

Narrator: Curlylocks has some of Father Bear's pizza.

Curlylocks: This pizza is too cold.

Narrator: Then Curlylocks has some of Mother Bear's pizza.

Curlylocks: This pizza is too hot.

Narrator: Then Curlylocks has some of Baby Bear's pizza.

Curlylocks: I love this pizza.
It is just right!

Narrator: Then Curlylocks gets in Father Bear's bed.

Curlylocks: This bed is too hard.

Narrator: Then Curlylocks gets in Mother Bear's bed.

Curlylocks: This bed is too soft.

Narrator: Then Curlylocks gets in Baby Bear's bed.

Curlylocks: I love this bed. It is just right!

Narrator: Then the three bears come back!

Father Bear: Someone has been eating my pizza!

Mother Bear: Someone has been eating my pizza!

Baby Bear: Someone has been eating my pizza and has eaten it all!

Father Bear: Someone has been sleeping in my bed!

Mother Bear: Someone has been sleeping in my bed!

Baby Bear: Someone has been sleeping in my bed – and here she is!

Curlylocks: Help! Help!

15

Narrator: So, Curlylocks runs home, and the three bears have some cake.

Three Bears: Mmmm!